MURDER BY DECAPITATION

NIKI DUPRE SHORT STORIES BOOK 11

JIM RILEY

To the Most Beautiful

You Always Were

You Always Will Be

MYSTERIES BY JIM RILEY

Hawk Theriot & Kristi Blocker full-length Mysteries

Murder in the Atchafalaya

Murder in Lake Palourde

Murder by Rougarou

Hawk Theriot & Kristi Blocker Short Story Mysteries

Murder at the Haunted House

Murder in the Cemetery

Wade Dalton & Sam Cates full-length Mysteries

The Girl in the Woods

Murder by Moccasin

Stranded in the Swamp

Wade Dalton & Sam Cates Short Story Mysteries

The Philandering Father

Murder for Lease

Murder and Rubber Chicken

Murder of the Mayor

Niki Dupre full-length Mysteries

Murder on Spirit Island

Murder at Tiger Eye

Murder & Billy Bailey

Murder in Louisiana Politics

Murder Under the Sun

Murder Goes to the Dogs

Murder for Peace

Murder &Needles

Niki Dupre Short Story Mysteries

Murder in the Cards

Murder of the Sheriff

Murder on Autopilot

Murder With a Bang

Murder for Art

Murder of the Banker

Murder at the Washateria

Murder on Loan

Murder Explodes with a Bang

Murder by Mistake

Murder is a Weighty Matter

Murder by Decapitation

CHAPTER ONE

———————————

SOMETHING WAS WRONG. Every strawberry blonde hair on the back of Niki's neck stood erect. She peered into the darkness. The young girl who called her earlier was nowhere in sight. A girl with a Hispanic accent. She told Niki she was about to be killed by Hector Gomez.

The girl had told the private detective where to find her. Not a pretty side of the state capitol of Louisiana. It was close to the Riverfront. Just enough distance from the mighty Mississippi to form a playground for the drug gangs and others with violent propensities.

This was one of those. A termite-infested building with the walls on the brink of collapsing. No lights shown from inside. Only blackness. Niki thought about the flashlight she always kept in the Ford Explorer. After a brief consideration, she opted to keep both hands free.

"Juanita," Niki called. "Are you here?"

Dead silence.

"Juanita. It's Niki Dupre. You called me."

More silence.

Niki took a step toward the door that stood ajar. Her senses became more acute. The detective's right hand rested on the butt of the S & W .38 revolver. It was holstered in the small of her back.

Two more steps, and the long-legged detective stopped.

She tried to pierce the blackness inside the building. For a second, she regretted leaving the flashlight. She pulled out the revolver. She waited.

If it was a trap, Niki didn't want to spring it. In her experience, street thugs had little patience. They were the ones who surrounded Hector Gomez. The bottom of the barrel. The kind of men who would sell their little sisters or their daughters into prostitution without a tinge of remorse.

Her ploy worked. A guy behind the door shuffled his feet. The sound wasn't loud, but it was enough to reveal the location of Niki's attackers. She assumed at least two were waiting. Maybe three. She settled on two. Hector Gomez didn't know her well.

Niki had earned the designation of Weapons Master in Kempo, the ancient Chinese martial art.

She was an expert in guns, long blades, short knives, long shafts, three-section rods, and nunchucks. She had proven capable of disarming a fellow while utilizing any of these weapons.

Taking a deep breath, she exploded into action.

CHAPTER TWO

The door slammed backward into the closest attacker. Niki rolled with a kick to the other side next to the wall. Shots from a small-caliber pistol tore into the door, the walls, the ceiling, and the floor.

The gunman had no idea where Niki disappeared. He sprayed the entire room with bullets. All seventeen shots. In frustration, he looked at the empty pistol.

Niki's foot caught him along his eyebrows. His head whipped backward and he tumbled over, his body stiff as a wet rag.

The private investigator wasted no time looking behind the door. That thug wasn't able to accomplish his assigned task.

The first man stumbled out. He held a Glock 9mm in one hand, while his other hand wiped blood from his nose and his mouth. He didn't look for Niki, assured his partner had completed their given tasks. He could not have been more wrong.

Niki landed an up-kick on the tip of the thug's chin. His head snapped back. She drove a straight kick to the middle of his throat. Niki heard the cartilage crunch.

The fellow dropped, gasping and grabbing at his neck. No matter how hard he tried, the precious oxygen could not travel to his lungs.

Niki turned back to the gunmen from before. He stirred with great pain, and reached for a knife handle that extended from his boot. Just as he grabbed the hilt, Niki smashed her foot into his elbow. He would need surgery before using it again. Niki grabbed his knife and tossed it toward a corner.

"Who are you?" she demanded.

The man mumbled a few curse words in Spanish. Niki put a foot on his injured elbow and pressed. He yelled as loud as he could.

"Shut up," Niki said. "You're supposed to be a man."

The guy rolled over, holding his right elbow with his left hand. He quit screaming and cursed again.

"I want a lawyer," he said in English.

"That's great," Niki responded. "I want some ice cream. Unfortunately, we'll both be disappointed."

"I know my rights. I want a lawyer."

Niki kicked his elbow again. Not hard. Just enough to elicit more screaming and cursing.

"Now that we're past that, tell me who you are."

The thug writhed on the floor. "Where is Artillio?"

"Do you mean Artie? He's over there. He's having a little trouble catching his breath. You will, too, if I don't get answers to my questions. Who are you?"

"Jesus."

"That wasn't hard, Jesus. Who sent you to kill me?"

"I can't ... He'll kill me."

"Guess what, Jesus. If you don't give me a name, the right one, he won't have that opportunity."

"You don't understand."

"I believe I do," Niki said. "I already know the name. I just want to hear you confirm it."

Jesus groaned more. Then he uttered a single word. "Hector."

CHAPTER THREE

Niki waited for the deputies outside by the SUV. She didn't want to get trapped by reinforcements. But, out in the lot, she could see trouble before it came. The first squad car arrived in less than four minutes.

"Are you the one who called?" the first deputy asked.

Niki nodded. "I'm Niki Dupre. You'll find one body inside and one guy with plastic cuffs. They tried to kill me."

"I need your weapon, ma'am," the deputy said.

Niki handed the revolver to him. "I didn't shoot either one."

The deputy paused, slightly confused. "Do you have a knife in your possession, ma'am?"

"I don't have one. There is one in the corner. It belongs to the guy whoI's still alive."

"Please, sit in the back of our car until we get this all sorted out."

Niki obeyed. She slipped into the backseat of the squad car. There were no door handles. She was trapped and became a bystander.

The talkative deputy went inside, using a flashlight. The second one waited outside. He drew his gun and switched his attention between Niki and his partner. Another vehicle drove up. Niki didn't bother to look, assuming it would be another squad car. That is, until its back door flung wide open.

CHAPTER FOUR

"WHAT THE HELL are you doing in there?" Samson Mayeaux roared. The massive cop was the Chief of Homicide for East Baton Rouge Parish. He'd known Niki since the day she was born. When Niki's parents were murdered when she was sixteen, she moved in with Samson and his wife, Liz.

"I killed a man," Niki said. "He and his partner tried to kill me."

"Why?"

"Hector Gomez. I ... uh, interviewed one of his lieutenants. I don't believe he appreciated the results."

"That was the Morales guy, huh? The one who was beheaded. We only found his body."

"That's the one. Hector wants to do the same to me. This was his first attempt."

"Did either guy admit that?" Samson asked.

"The one who's still alive. His name is Jesus."

"I won't ask how you got him to confess."

"He was in pain," Niki said, grinning. "He thought he was about to die. I didn't dissuade him."

"Was he afraid he was about to die from his wounds or something else?"

"Look," Niki said as she looked around Samson's girth, "the deputy is coming back out."

Samson turned to greet him. The deputy showed great deference to the Chief, as did everyone on the force. Samson's reputation demanded it. His physical presence demanded it. His aura of dominance demanded it.

"Good evening, sir," the deputy said. "I wasn't aware you would come out on this call."

"I bet," Samson roared. "Otherwise, you wouldn't have locked up my little girl in your car."

"Sir." The deputy instinctively took a step back. "I followed procedure. I had to contain all parties until I knew the events that took place."

"And you found ...?"

"Two bodies."

"Whoa!" Samson turned to Niki. "Little Girl, I thought you told me you only killed one guy tonight."

"I did," Niki replied. "The second shooter was still alive when I walked outside."

"Excuse me, sir," the deputy interjected. "There is

one live perp with his hands cuffed. There are also two dead bodies."

Samson turned to Niki. The private investigator shrugged.

The deputy continued. "We found one adult male with his throat crushed ..."

"That one is mine," Niki interrupted. "I killed him."

"The other is a preteen, as far as I can tell. It's hard to be certain with her head missing."

CHAPTER FIVE

"DID YOU IDENTIFY THE GIRL?" Niki asked.

Samson, and Donna Cross joined Niki in her favorite restaurant, Linda's Chicken & Fish, the following day. Samson was one of the few people who could come close to Donna's voracious appetite. The difference was he weighed in at three hundred and fifty pounds. Donna was an hourglass blonde. No matter how much she ate, and it was more than Niki could fathom, Donna maintained her symmetrical measurements. Samson kept the shape of a blimp.

"Yep," Samson said between bites of fried catfish fillets. "Her name was Juanita, just like she told you. We can't find any connection to Hector Gomez."

"It doesn't matter," Niki said. "She was only a kid."

"Eleven." Samson said as he eyed one of Donna's

triple cheeseburgers. "Was gonna be twelve next month."

"What she tortured?" Niki asked as Donna moved her food a bit farther out of Samson's reach.

"Do you mean other than being decapitated?" Samson asked.

Niki nodded. She saw Samson's hand sliding toward a basket of onion rings Donna had not yet moved.

"She was raped," Samson said as he grabbed the basket.

Donna jumped up and fell on his colossal arm. It did no good. Samson emptied half the basket before returning the rest of the onion rings to the blonde.

"Thank you, Donna," he said. "I appreciate you sharing."

"No problem," Donna grinned. Samson also grinned. He saw the stack of Boudin links the curvaceous blonde took while he was stealing her onion rings. "Good job."

"Why did he have to do that? The one-million-dollar contract he put out was for my head. Not Juanita's."

"I believe he planned to lure you to that building to do exactly the same to you," Samson said.

"But his beef is with me."

"He wanted to send two messages. Really, one message to two different audiences," the huge cop said while eyeing the bucket of chicken in front of Donna.

"Who are the two audiences?" Donna asked, raising a fork above Samson's enormous paw.

"Niki and the people like her are one. She tried to interfere with the way Hector did business."

"And the other?" Donna kept the fork ready to attack.

"My guess is somebody stiffed him. Might have been a drug deal, gambling debts, or refusal to pay for his protection. Hector can't afford to let that happen without a proper response." He withdrew his hand.

"That makes sense," Niki said. "Poor little Juanita was the daughter of some schmuck who got into debt with Hector. He couldn't pay, so Juanita did with her life. I'm not growing fond of Hector."

"Unfortunately, we can't touch Gomez," Samson said.

"Why not?" Niki asked. "I told you what Jesus told me."

"And that constitutes hearsay," Samson said. "You know that from all the time you spent in a courtroom."

"So, why don't you ask Jesus to repeat it? I'm sure you can make a deal with him."

"I wish we could. It's no longer possible."

"Why not?"

"He was killed last night. The morning guards found his head stuffed in a toilet."

Niki lost her appetite.

CHAPTER SIX

Niki set out on a path to bring Hector down. The private investigator could not attack him directly. His estate was more like a fortress than a residence. The ten thousand square-foot home was surrounded by twenty acres of dense forests and bramble. The few trails through the woods were littered with traps and snares for the unwary.

The detective opted to hit him where the money flowed. She decided to pinch Hector's cash flow. She might not be able to clog the pipeline entirely, but she could severely hamper the flow through it.

She began with the easiest. Once a month, three goons hired by Hector made the round of small businesses. If the owner didn't pay, his company would suffer, maybe by fire, theft, or by a loss of customers. So, in one way or another, Hector hurt the owner.

The trio of thugs rotated through the different minority communities. On this particular week, they patrolled Government Street. Niki spotted the beefed-up sedan twenty minutes after arriving.

They parked outside a pay-day loan office. Niki had no sympathy for these outfits that charged exorbitant rates. Once, she looked into the industry. Most of their loans were to repeat customers. The same borrower might have three or four different loans at the same time.

Two Hispanic men and a big fellow that looked Russian to Niki made up the trio. The Russian acted as the leader by default. He was twice the size of his companions. One Hispanic man was short and fat. The other, short and skinny. Neither looked physically menacing.

However, she saw the bulges under their shirts. Both carried semiautomatic pistols. Niki had more trouble discerning where the Russian hid his gun.

His girth was one problem. The other was a padded belt around his entire girth. The money belt. That was the thing the detective wanted. The only problem was those three thugs standing in her way.

CHAPTER SEVEN

Niki followed them to the next small business, a pawn shop advertising the purchase of gold and silver jewelry. This was another business for which the investigator held little sympathy.

The rates offered by pawnshops bordered on breaking the usury laws of the state. They also did little to verify that the items being pawned were legit. Many kids on the street made money stealing jewelry before hocking it.

The trio pulled in. The Russian was in the front seat. The skinny Mexican drove. The little fat guy looked like a trailing puppy.

Niki waited for them to go inside before exiting her white Ford Explorer. Her fingers automatically fell to the butt of the S & W .38 tucked in the small of her back.

She walked inside.

There was no sign of Hector's thugs. Only a young boy, barely in his teens, minded the counter. *Must be the owner's son*, Niki thought. The kid could be an issue. The last thing the investigator wanted was for harm to come to an innocent child in her battle with Hector.

Collateral damage was one thing. When that damage came in the form of innocent kids, Niki drew the line. The skirmish could not take place in the storefront.

She walked up to the kid. "Are they in the office or the warehouse?"

The boy looked over his shoulder and drew a short breath before looking down a short hall. There were only two doors. One had to lead to the office. The other, to the warehouse. She preferred the warehouse. It would provide more room to use Kempo.

That hope died when she opened the first door on the left.

CHAPTER EIGHT

THE OWNER LOOKED like he was in his mid-forties. It was hard to tell with the blood on his lip and his face contorted in pain. The Russian twisted the owner's left arm at an odd angle.

When she opened the door, the four men looked at her.

"Uh, oh," she said. "This isn't the bathroom."

"Get out of here, bitch," the Russian said with a thick accent. "You not see nothing."

Niki didn't back out. Instead, she took a step inside. She stared at the pawnshop owner. At least, that's what she wanted them to think. The private investigator sized up her competition.

The most dangerous of the three was the Russian. He was busy torturing the owner. Of the two

Mexicans, Niki feared the skinny one most. The fat one trembled already. He would be slow to react.

"I tell you get out of here," the Russian said.

"He seems to be in pain." Niki nodded at the owner. "Maybe I can help him."

The Russian looked confused. *Goon Trading for Dummies* apparently lacked a chapter outlining this scenario. He didn't know what to do. He looked at the two Mexicans.

"'Take her out," he said.

It was music to Niki's ears. The Russian didn't tell his companions to kill her. Their instructions were to merely escort her out of the building and reinforce her lapse of memory. The detective loved the odds.

The skinny one acted first. This was no surprise to Niki. When he reached for her arm, the strawberry blonde burst into action. With one kick, the skinny Mexican was on the floor with a broken jaw.

Without hesitation, the martial arts expert spun and smashed a foot into the fat Mexican's stomach. The air gushed out of him like a balloon. Even as the man bent over, Niki's knee delivered a numbing uppercut that laid him out on the floor.

Niki turned to the Russian. He wrenched the owner's arms again, his brain unable to absorb what his eyes saw. He stood there stunned, presenting an inviting target for Niki. She did not immediately take this opportunity to kick his ass—for good reason.

CHAPTER NINE

Niki waited. She wanted to talk to the big guy first. She needed him to deliver a message to Hector. The private investigator wanted the gangster to know for certain who the fly was in his ointment.

"What's your name?" She asked.

"Karl," the big man responded.

"Do you work for Hector Gomez?"

"I do many things."

"Are you shaking down this business on behalf of Hector?"

A shrug.

"That's okay. I already know the truth. Hand over the money belt around your waist."

Alarm showed for the first time in the Russian's eyes. It was one thing for this skinny woman to kick the hell out of the hired help. It was another for her to demand the money without holding a gun.

He smiled. Karl Brzezinski had been in many fights. Too many to remember. Some were against one opponent. Some against two. A few against more. He had never lost. He had beaten macho men. He had beaten men armed with guns and knives. In his consideration, this lean lady didn't stand a chance.

Karl laughed. The absurdity of a girl one-third his weight battling him was funny. This was a moment he could relay to his vodka-drinking comrades.

"Why you not leave? I not want to hurt you."

"Give me the money belt and tell me you will get out of the protection racket. Then, I'll leave."

The laughter turned into a roar. He couldn't believe the demands from this girl. They were ludicrous.

"Nyet. You leave, and I not hurt you."

Niki grew tired of the conversation. She had only one more thing to tell the big Russian before she broke both his knees, two ribs, and fractured his lower mandible.

"Tell Hector Niki did this."

CHAPTER TEN

Neither Niki nor the pawnshop owner wanted to call the police. The owner didn't want them to know he had participated in a protection ring. Not even as a victim. If he did, that might mean testifying against Hector Gomez. Pure suicide.

Niki had a different reason. She didn't want Samson and his deputies getting in her way. Stopping the three goons at the pawnshop was only the first skirmish. The war was in the offing.

With the help of the owner, she rolled the Russian back and forth until she could wrangle the money belt from his body. Inside, she found one hundred and thirteen thousand dollars. Not a bad morning take for the trio of thugs. Niki doubted that all three of these together made that much in a year.

The detective contemplated the amount they

would take over a whole month. Since the day was less than half over, she assumed a quarter of a million each day. With more than twenty working days each month, Hector gathered five million in revenue from this one operation. He would not appreciate any interference.

"Do you need help with these guys?" Niki pointed at the three injured men.

"My son and I will take care of them," the owner said. "What do I do if they come back again?"

"Call me." She pulled out a business card and handed it over. "It doesn't matter if it's day or night."

"But they will kill me while you're on the way."

"I don't think so," Niki said. "That's why I told the big guy my name. He'll come after me first."

"Aren't you scared?"

Niki sighed. She knew the possibility of her early demise had increased dramatically with her actions. However, she had faith. Her guardian angels were omnipresent. They never left her side. As long as she fought against the agents of evil, they would let no harm come to her.

"I'm not scared of Hector Gomez," Niki said. "I'm scared of the damage he can do before I stop him."

"I wouldn't want to be in your shoes."

"Why not?" Niki looked down at her sneakers. "They're the most comfortable pair I own."

CHAPTER ELEVEN

Niki didn't want to lose the element of surprise. Hector might have heard of the incident at the pawn-shop, but she doubted it. There was one disadvantage to being a cruel gangster. Nobody wanted to be the bearer of bad news.

She hopped on the interstate and crossed the new Mississippi River bridge. The crew could be in the closest city, Port Allen, or any of the numerous riverside towns. If she was unlucky, they could be as far north as New Roads, another thirty minutes north of her present position.

The investigator had no description of the men or their car. She could only assume Hector would stick to the same pattern of the three goons. Sending only one would mean he would skim off the top. With two, it was possible. With three, one of them would turn into a snitch.

Thirty minutes later, the investigator was about to turn north when she spotted three men coming out of a small café. The biggest one, a white male, stuffed green bills into a satchel. Niki followed them.

They stopped next at an auto repair shop. When the other two men, one Black and one Hispanic, followed the white guy into the garage, the detective saw the bulges of their weapons under their shirts. This time, she saw the weapons on all three. The Caucasian was not nearly as bulky as the Russian.

That didn't mean he was less dangerous. He had a confident stride in his movements. From that, Niki figured the white guy was in fear of no one.

But, he made a mistake. The man carried the satchel in his dominant hand, the one on his right. To pull his gun, the guy would first have to drop the bag or transfer it to his left hand. Judging by how hard he grasped the handle, there was no way he would consider dropping it.

Niki waited until the men were inside, then she exited the SUV. She needed to catch them off guard.

CHAPTER TWELVE

No TORTURE TOOK place in the garage. Niki found that out from the pawnshop owner who had refused to pay more than a thousand a week to the thugs. They were in the process of convincing him when Niki had entered. After the event, Niki paid him fifty thousand from the money belt to make up for his losses.

Either the repair shop owner agreed with the increased fees, or the thugs were not asking for them. He and the trio of henchmen stood in the back of the garage out of sight from the customers. They greeted each other like old friends.

At first, Niki thought she might have been mistaken. Could she be on the wrong track? She wasn't sure until she saw the owner open the till. He raised the bill drawer and reached underneath.

When his hand reappeared, it held a bundle of green bills.

Niki didn't know how much the bundle represented. She knew, however, that she had found Hector's men. Since the victim was in no immediate danger, she let them come to her.

The detective turned and pretended to be inspecting a stack of new tires. Automobile parts held no particular interest to Niki. Tires were at the bottom of that list. However, she looked like a connoisseur of black rubber when the men approached. When she bent over, one whistled and made a lewd remark.

Niki whirled. She lashed out with a kick to the man's sternum. The Black man hurled backward. Unable to catch his balance, he toppled to the floor.

"Wasn't no call for that," the white man said. "Earl was just playing with you."

Neither of the remaining two seemed to sense danger. The Hispanic guy laughed at his fallen colleague. The big Caucasian glared at Niki. The satchel remained in his right hand.

"I'm not playing," Niki said as she drove a foot into the Hispanic's ear. He fell to the side.

The big white man finally figured out the peril he faced. He began to transfer the satchel to his left hand. It never made it that far.

Niki's foot cratered his right knee. Her other foot broke every ligament and tendon in his left. He fell face forward, trying to get to his pistol. The effort came to a halt when she broke the ulna in his right arm.

The white man struggled to his feet. He wasn't on them for long. A kick across the bridge of his nose put him down and out.

Niki picked up the suitcase. She walked back to where the stunned garage owner stood.

"How much of this is yours?" she asked.

"I pay them a thousand a week. I gave them one thousand."

Niki pulled ten one hundred dollar bills from the bag.

"Here. You don't ever have to pay them again. Hector Gomez is going out of business."

The big guy moaned, lying on the floor. Niki knelt close to his ear.

"Tell Hector Niki did this."

Then she rose, spun, and kicked. The guy would be unable to tell anyone anything for a while. The detective collected their guns and left carrying the satchel.

CHAPTER THIRTEEN

Niki had an option of three targets that night. Hector dealt in gambling, prostitution, and drugs in addition to the protection racket. She had no leads for the gambling center. The prostitution business was highly decentralized. Pimps ran the whores in different sections of town. Collection was made weekly by Hector's men. The time and location varied.

That left the drug business. While also decentralized, there was one difference between it and prostitution. Hector operated a warehouse that acted as the center of distribution. His lieutenants gathered the necessary products every night for distribution to the street dealers.

It ran like any business selling widgets. The individual street guy never knew too much. The possibility of theft by them, robbery by outsiders, or busts by the narcotics squad were too risky. Instead, Hector's managers at the warehouse gave the lieutenants just enough for one night.

This approach also kept an artificial lid on the supply. With the demand rising and the supply stagnant, the prices Hector's organization charged kept increasing.

The only problem was that Niki didn't know the location of the warehouse. She doubted that any of the street guys knew it either. Only the lieutenants passing out drugs to the street dealers would know.

CHAPTER FOURTEEN

Niki drove up to a dealer on Choctaw Drive. She rolled her window down. The dealer, accustomed to the white folks coming to the neighborhood for drugs, strode to the window.

He was no more than a boy. Niki estimated his age to be fifteen or sixteen. Hard lines already crossed his face. On this night, he grinned. He had a customer earlier than usual. She was driving a fine SUV, so he knew she could afford the best. He might not have the best, but there was no reason for her to know.

"I need a quarter kilo," she said.

"Damn, bitch. You think I carry that around?"

"How soon can you get it?"

"Tomorrow," the boy said. "You gotta pay tonight."

"How much?"

The boy quoted a price that shocked the private investigator. She wasn't in the usual market for cocaine, and had no idea it was that expensive. She pulled the cash out of the satchel she had obtained earlier.

"Here," Niki said, "but I want it tonight."

"Can't do it, bitch. You gotta wait your turn."

"I'll pay you the same amount again if I can get it tonight. It's an emergency."

The thought of doubling the already exorbitant price she paid was too much for the greedy kid. He reached for the money. Niki grabbed his little finger and bent it back to the point of snapping.

"If you don't get it tonight, I'll be back. I'll also be angry. You won't like me when I'm angry."

The kid screamed and yanked his hand back.

"What did you do that for, bitch?"

"You had the look of deceit in your eyes. I didn't like it. How long before I can pick up the stuff?"

"One hour," the kid said while examining his hurt finger. "If you're late, you lose your money."

"You just have my order ready. I'll be here."

Niki drove off, letting the money flutter to the ground. If the kid was busy picking it up, he wouldn't notice her pull into a vacant parking lot.

CHAPTER FIFTEEN

THE LIEUTENANT DROVE A VOLKSWAGEN BUG. It was a vehicle Niki would never have expected. She watched as the guy in the Bug collected the money. He handed a small package to the kid. The exchange took less than thirty seconds. The VW made a U-turn on Choctaw and went back to the same direction from which it came.

Niki waited for it to pass before pulling out on Choctaw. She left her lights off until the vehicle got on the I-110 stretch. The detective blended in with the other traffic. It was not rush hour. However, there were still plenty of cars on the interstate. At times, Niki thought the VW had taken an exit without her noticing. She would then see it again.

I-110 merged with I-10 at the base of the Mississippi River bridge. The Bug took the next exit that led to the riverfront. Niki knew there were dozens of old warehouses along the mighty river. Most of them had been abandoned for years.

Two miles from the bridge, the VW pulled off the road. An old warehouse stood next to the pavement. That was not the destination. Another building stood behind the massive warehouse. It was smaller and completely hidden from prying eyes. Niki had driven past this location dozens of times without realizing the existence of the smaller building.

Instead of following the VW to the distribution center, Niki pulled up on the levee separating the river from the road. She killed the engine and waited. After ten minutes, she assumed the SUV had drawn no special attention.

The long-legged detective eased out of the Explorer and walked down the levee and across the road. She sneaked fifty yards past the big warehouse and entered an alley between it and the next one.

The smaller building bustled with activity. The lieutenants made special rows of large quantities.

A chain-link fence separated the compound from the other buildings. Two men dressed in security uniforms stood at the gate. Each was armed with a Glock 17. Both weapons were strapped in their holsters. Niki had to devise an ad hoc plan of assault.

CHAPTER SIXTEEN

T HE STRAWBERRY BLONDE decided against a frontal attack through the gate. That was where Hector's men would expect a raid to originate. She saw something that made her heart sink. A squad car with two deputies pulled up to the gate.

The two guards waved at the driver and opened the gate. Niki realized this was not a raid. The car stopped in front of a roll-up door. A walk-through door on the side opened. A man walked out, holding a brown paper bag. The deputy on the passenger side got out and took the bag. He placed it in the trunk of the squad car.

Niki's gut twisted in furious knots. Those two cops were taking bribes. She couldn't tell if the bag contained drugs or money. It made no difference. They were deliberately turning their heads to drug trafficking. There was no way she could call on the East Baton Rouge Sheriff's Department for help.

She memorized the unit number of the car. She also paid attention to the deputy who she could see. White. Five feet, ten inches. Pudgy, but not fat. Brown hair. A slight limp as though he had sprained his left ankle. If nothing else, she would make sure these two received their just reward–if she lived through the night.

She watched as a squad car backed up and turned around. The private investigator felt the bile rise in her throat as the driver honked and waved at the two guards. She wanted to go back to the Explorer and chase down those traitors. They were worse than the drug dealers. They pretended to be on the side of law and order.

She remembered her mission. There would be plenty of time to deal with the crooked deputies later.

CHAPTER SEVENTEEN

WITH THE EASE OF AN ACROBAT, Niki scaled the chain-link fence. She belly-crawled to the nearest window at the end of the warehouse. It was about chest level. The height wasn't the problem. The thick grime on it was.

No matter how hard she tried, the view inside was obscured by the filth on the panes. She heard the creak of the door not ten feet away. She was on the wrong side. The guy would be able to see her before he stepped outside.

Niki pulled her jacket over her chin and lowered her face. She strode toward the door. When the guy stepped out, he pulled a cigarette from the pack he carried. He paid no attention, assuming the investigator was another worker finishing a smoke break.

Niki grabbed him and hurled the smoker forward

onto his face. He tried to scream. A foot to the side of his head stifled that attempt.

The unconscious man wore a Levi jacket, jeans, a T-shirt, and a sombrero. The large hat had flown off his head with Niki's initial jerk.

Both the jacket and sombrero were a size too big. That worked to Niki's advantage. She folded her long strawberry blonde mane under the hat. The sleeves covered her delicate hands and manicured nails.

She figured the man would be out at least thirty minutes. If she had not completed her task during that time, it would matter little. She would already be through with the mission, or she would be dead.

CHAPTER EIGHTEEN

Niki stepped into the building after dragging the smoker into the darkness. No sense in letting another nicotine addict discover him and raise the alarm.

She took an immediate right behind a stack of brick-sized packages. The whole stack was sixty feet wide, eighty feet long, and eighteen feet high. Niki couldn't fathom the street value of that one pile of dope.

There were many more stacks. Not all of them had the same size and shape as the first, but all were piled high. Niki figured the value of the contents of all the packages ran into the high eight figures. And that was a conservative guess.

Even as she had planned to take away Hector's distribution center, the investigator never dreamed it was this big. No wonder the gangster could afford to pay off the cops. The two she had seen were probably the tip of the iceberg.

"Hey, Bud." The voice came from behind her. "You're supposed to be working, not hiding."

Niki had no choice. She put the man down with one well-placed kick. She shoved his body between two rows of packages. No one would be able to see it from the end of the aisle.

Niki went to the walkway at the end by the wall. From there, she had an excellent view all the way to the other end. The piles of drugs prevented the investigator from seeing across.

Suddenly, a white guy stepped out in front of her.

"Who the hell are you? That's José's hat."

Another swift kick. Another drug dealer down. She dragged him out of the aisle, thankful for the three-hour workouts every morning. She breathed normally when she stepped back into the aisle.

Halfway down, the stacks were lower. Niki climbed one, wanting to get a view of her surroundings. Two guards stood inside the door, each armed within an AK-47 assault rifle. The guards were not on full alert. One drank a cup of coffee while listening to the other. The joke must have been funny. Both laughed.

That was the bad news. The good news was Niki counted only five more workers and one supervisor. The odds, which seemed overwhelming, moved in the investigator's favor. She smiled as she climbed down. *I might actually pull this off,* she thought.

Niki came up behind one worker who was busy loading little plastic bags into a larger brown one. The brown bag was similar to the one the deputies took earlier.

The poor worker had no chance. Niki stacked plastic bags on top of him when she finished, hiding the body from view.

The other four workers went down one by one. That left only the lieutenant and the two guards inside. Two guards remained at the gate. The investigator's game plan changed.

CHAPTER NINETEEN

SHE WAITED until another driver arrived. The last supervisor inside accepted a wad of cash from him. Niki watched the inside man stuff bills in an unlocked safe. Bad move on his part.

The driver left after receiving his cut of the action. That left only the manager inside and two guards within her view.

The lieutenant called out in English, "Hey, where did everybody go? You can't all take a break at the same time."

He got no response. All the workers were in dreamland through no fault of their own. They could not answer their boss.

Disgusted, the man strode toward the back door. Niki ambushed him fifteen feet from the exit. She couldn't afford to let him yell out to the guards. However, she needed him alive. He was the one who would deliver the message to Hector Gomez.

A quick kick to his throat, and he went quiet. The blow wasn't hard enough to crush his windpipe. He clutched his throat and crumpled to the ground.

Niki knelt beside the injured lieutenant. He looked at her while gasping for air.

"Tell Hector Niki did this."

She spun and drove her foot into the man's temple. She didn't want him to interfere with the next step of her plan.

CHAPTER TWENTY

THE TWO GUARDS remained overly casual. Niki's problem was the gap between them and cover. The investigator thought about shooting both. Nevertheless, she rejected the idea. The outside guards would be alerted, and would call Hector. She didn't want him to know of her intrusion yet.

The private investigator hunkered down in the third row from the front of the building. Pulling the sombrero down and the oversized jacket up, almost no skin could be seen.

"Help me," she called in a soft tone.

The two guards heard her. They quit chatting and strained to hear more. Neither rose.

"Help me," Niki whimpered again.

The younger one jumped to his feet. "Somebody is hurt. You stay here while I check it out."

He walked toward the sound, the AK-47 slung over his shoulder. The youngster anticipated a crew member had tested the product and could no longer function. It wouldn't be the first time a worker couldn't resist the temptation.

His job was not to administer punishment. He would turn the poor peon over to Hector's men. That would be the last time the worker stole from anyone.

He saw the huddled figure in the middle of the aisle. It sat on the floor, doubled over.

"Hey, Pedro," the guard yelled. He was pretty sure that was not the man's name. He called all Mexicans *Pedro*. It was easier than learning their names.

Pedro did not respond. No verbal communication. No acknowledgment that the guard existed. The uniformed man walked up and nudged the huddled guy with the top of his boot.

"Hey, Pedro. What's wrong?"

Nikki's hand missed his throat, because he ducked to grab what he thought was a worker. The blow caught him full on his mouth. It wasn't sufficient to keep them quiet. The kick from a sitting position solved the problem. He tumbled over and fell against a pile of drugs.

Niki wasted no more time on him. She heard footsteps running at them. She slid the dagger from the sheath at her ankle.

The blade flew through the air as the other guard appeared in the opening. The sharp instrument buried up to the hilt in his chest. The astonished man looked down at it, then up at Niki.

The strawberry blonde almost felt sorry for the guy. He was only doing his job. But his job was guarding a warehouse full of drugs that killed people and wrecked the lives of others. She reasoned his death was for a just cause.

Niki raced to the open safe. There was too much money for her to carry free-handed. The investigator dumped a duffle bag full of dope and filled it with bills. She had to repeat the process.

There were still a few bills remaining when she toted the heavy bags toward the back door. It was time to implement the final step in her plan.

CHAPTER TWENTY-ONE

She stored the bags away in the rear compartment of the SUV. The detective took out a burner phone and sneaked back down the levy and across the street. This time, however, she did not cross the chain-link fence.

She dialed the emergency number. The operator answered.

"There's a gunfight. One man is dead," she said, before giving the address of the warehouse. "Please send help."

"Who is this?" The operator asked.

Niki hung up and waited. She didn't have to wait long. The same squad car that had previously been there drove up with its lights flashing and siren blaring.

A brief conversation at the front gate seemed to

remove the panic from the situation. Niki was scared the two deputies would leave too soon. Instead, they drove through the gate up to the building. Niki waited for them to get out of the car and enter the warehouse. Neither cop seemed overly concerned.

As soon as they were out of sight, Niki aimed the S & W .38 revolver. It was a long shot for a small-caliber gun. The detective was confident.

Two shots fired in rapid succession. A brief pause and two more. Niki took one glance at the two flat tires before sprinting back to the levy. She redialed the emergency number.

"The cops that came to the warehouse are under fire. You guys need to send back-up before they get killed."

Soon, the whole parking lot around the warehouse was filled with flashing lights and sirens.

CHAPTER TWENTY-TWO

Niki drove down the levy and parked the SUV outside the chain-link fence. She knew everything inside it would be part of the crime scene. She didn't want the cops to discover the two duffle bags.

She spotted a familiar face. Okay—she saw the immense profile of Samson Mayeaux before she saw his face. His physical girth was hard to miss.

"Hey, Little Girl," the Chief of Homicide called. He used the same pet name he had since the day Niki was born.

"Hey, Samson. What's happening here?"

"We hit the jackpot!" Samson beamed. "We found the central warehouse of Hector Gomez. I was beginning to think it didn't exist."

"That ought to get you a promotion. Heck, I

might be calling you Mr. Mayor-President after the next election."

Samson snorted. "I'll leave politics to the politicians. This is the strangest situation, though."

"What strange about it?" Niki asked while trying to hide her amusement.

"We got an anonymous tip. Said our men were under attack. When I got here, somebody had shot out the tires of their car."

"If I were you, I'd look in the truck of that car," Niki said. "Those two cops might be dirty."

Samson opened his mouth to say something, then closed it. He looked at Niki with a knowing glance. She smiled and gave him her most angelic expression. The big cop didn't buy it. He snorted and walked away.

"Martin," he yelled. "Come open your trunk."

Niki watched as the cop she had seen earlier stepped forward. Even in the darkness, the private investigator could see his whole body shaking.

"Why, Chief?" Martin whined. "What do you want?"

"I want to see what's inside that truck, Deputy. Now, open it up," Samson roared.

"Don't you need a warrant or something?" Martin asked.

"Not to open one of my cars, you idiot. Quit playing and hand me your keys."

Martin reluctantly relinquished the set of keys to

Samson. The mammoth Chief opened the trunk. Before picking up the bag, he donned a pair of latex gloves. When he opened it, he pulled out half a dozen plastic sacks.

Martin charged at Samson. Niki didn't react. Samson almost nonchalantly delivered a roundhouse to the deputy's head. The deputy dropped in his tracks.

"Arrest this garbage and his partner," he said.

After Samson handed off the evidence to a detective, he turned to talk to Niki. She was nowhere to be seen.

CHAPTER TWENTY-THREE

Niki was munching on a bran muffin when her cell phone rang. She had already completed the three hours of daily Kempo training. She had even finished the thirty-minute run and taken a shower. She was ready for another day of attacking Hector's businesses. The phone call changed her plans.

"Niki," she answered.

"This is Hector," the boy said.

Niki had no clue what Hector's voice sounded like. Her instincts told her this was it.

"Hello, Hector," she said pleasantly. "What can I do for you on this lovely day?"

"You have been a bad girl, Niki Dupre."

"What did you expect?" Niki laughed. "You sent your goons to kill me. You used a little girl named

Juanita, and then you beheaded her. How did you expect me to react?"

"I don't expect no reaction," Gomez said. "I expect you to be dead."

"And the girl? What did she do to you?"

"Her padre. He don't pay his debts, so I send him a message."

"And I'm sending you one, Hector. Mine caused you to lose billions of dollars."

"You will pay, Niki Dupre."

"Why don't you and I settle it? One on one. Just you and me."

"I've got a better idea. You bring back my money. Then I take your head."

"Gee, that sounds like a magnanimous offer on your part. Still, I think I'll decline."

"You are in no position to negotiate."

"Really," Niki laughed. "I believe I have over twenty million in cash you want back. I think that gives me the best hand."

"That's not true," Hector replied. "I have the wild-card. Hold on. I'll let you talk to her."

Niki's heart sank. Even before she heard Donna's voice, she knew Hector had kidnapped her best friend and business partner.

"Niki, don't do it," Donna screamed over the phone. "They're gonna kill me anyway!"

Niki heard the unmistakable sound of a fist hitting flesh. She wanted to vomit.

"Now, who has the best hand?" Hector asked.

"You do," Niki admitted. "If you touch one hair on her head, I'll hunt you down like the rabid skunk you are."

"Strong words for someone with no cards. I want my money, and I want you. I'll trade the whore for both."

"Deal," Niki said. "But I pick the time and the place."

"No problem," Hector replied. "I believe you are not foolish enough to call the cops. Your friend will be the first to die."

"You, and I mean *you*, Hector. You bring her to the BREC park in Central in one hour. It should be deserted at this time of the morning."

"Is that a demand, Niki Dupre?"

"It sure is. I want to tell you to your face what a lowlife you are before I die."

Niki hung up with Hector laughing on the other end.

CHAPTER TWENTY-FOUR

HECTOR'S MEN spread out and hid under cover around the park. One entered the men's room and raised a window and another climbed on top of the washroom. Two more hid in the woods behind the park.

The gangster dragged Donna to the bench in the center of the small recreation area. Hector had taped the hourglass blonde's mouth. He had secured her hands with plastic ties. Tears streamed down Donna's cheeks over her dimples. Her full lips quivered.

"It will be all over soon, Miss Cross. Don't fret."

Donna cursed as best she could through the tape.

Hector shoved her onto the bench. He pulled out a curved machete. The meaning was clear. Gomez looked around. The only sentry he saw was the man on the roof of the washroom.

The closest man to Niki in the woods didn't make a sound. The strawberry blonde slipped a hand over his mouth before slitting his throat. She wiped the blade on the thug's shirt. Without a sound, the detective slipped forty feet to the following sniper. She buried the knife up to the hilt where the spinal cord joined his neck. A quick death followed instant paralysis.

The next guy positioned himself inside the restroom. The long-legged investigator stepped inside without notice from the man on the roof. She ignored the stench. Hector's man knelt by the open window. He never looked back at Niki. A huge mistake on his part. It was his last. Coming out of the washroom, Niki paused. She went back inside. After grabbing a roll of toilet paper, she wiped her knife dry and felt the blade. It was still sharp.

Niki took two steps, clearing the hangover. She had a clear view of the rifleman on the roof. Even as the blade flew through the air, she raced toward the bench.

The rifleman's reflex from the impact of the knife between his shoulders made his finger twitch. The report from the gun filled the small park.

Hector reacted to the sound. He turned to look at the dying man on the roof. Niki flew at him like a missile. Her foot broke the wrist holding the machete. Hector howled as he dropped the blade and collapsed.

Niki stood over him. "Hello, Hector. At last, we meet."

"You bitch," he screamed. "I'll have your head!"

Niki picked up the curved blade.

"You can't even hold a knife, Hector. Your reign is over."

"I'll get you," he shrieked. "Even from jail, I'll kill you and your friend."

"That's what I was thinking," Niki said. "I don't mind you coming after me, but you took Donna. I won't allow that to happen again."

"You can't do nothing about it," Hector sneered.

The machete flashed. Hector's decapitated head hit the ground before his body collapsed.

"Yes," Niki spat out. "I can."

CHAPTER TWENTY-FIVE

The Police Benevolence Fund received a cashier's check for five million dollars. The reference simply said, "From Hector".

The Woman's Shelter in Baton Rouge received a similar one. Other organizations in the Metroplex also received donations. All were signed the same.

Hector Gomez's money was put to good use in the end. Niki smiled while eating Cajun fried chicken liver at Linda's.

THE END

Dear reader,

We hope you enjoyed reading *Murder By Decapitation*. Please take a moment to leave a review, even if it's a short one. Your opinion is important to us.

Discover more books by Jim Riley at https://www.nextchapter.pub/authors/jim-riley

Want to know when one of our books is free or discounted? Join the newsletter at http://eepurl.com/bqqB3H

Best regards,
Jim Riley and the Next Chapter Team

AUTHOR'S NOTES

Murder by Decapitation is the eleventh of over twenty short mysteries in the Niki Dupre series. It features the dynamic martial arts expert facing even more significant challenges.

I have taken a tremendous literary license with the geography and data of Baton Rouge and the surrounding areas. It is a beautiful city and a great way to experience Cajun culture. I live there and find it one of the most desirable places on earth if you enjoy the outdoors, excellent cuisine, and remarkable people.

There are so many people to thank:

My family, Linda, Josh, Dalton & Jade

David and Sara Sue

C D and Debbie Smith

My brother and sister-in-law, Bill & Pam

My sister, Debbie

My sister-in-law and her husband, Brenda & Jerry

The Sunday School class at Zoar Baptist

Jeff Trout and Chris Hall, two real men who stood beside me during my darkest hours. Jeff tried to teach me about Kempo, the ancient Chinese martial art. He soon found out I'm a slow learner.

Any mistakes, typos, and errors are my fault and mine alone. If you would like to get in touch with me, go to my website: http://jimriley.net

Thank you for reading **Murder by Decapitation**, and I hope you will also enjoy the rest of my books.

Murder By Decapitation
ISBN: 978-4-86752-905-8
Large Print

Published by
Next Chapter
1-60-20 Minami-Otsuka
170-0005 Toshima-Ku, Tokyo
+818035793528

9th August 2021